BIG MONTY AND THE PUMPED UP PRINCIPAL

BIG MONTY

and

THE PUMPED UP PRINCIPAL

BY

MATT MAXX

*Did you know that Big Monty Books were
made possible by over
150 people who made donations?*

*Here's a special thanks to our Patron School
Sponsor Donors:*

Ty Pinkins and Family

The Buys Family

Kyle and Susan Ridout

Jennifer Seltzer

Steve and Ellen Ramp

*Without these supporters,
Big Monty would never have gotten started
on his adventures!*

TABLE OF CONTENTS

Chapter 1   The Thinking Room and Two
              Wrongly Accused Dudes   1

Chapter 2   A Superior Substitute and
              One Weird Inmate   9

Chapter 3   A Sleep Fighter and an
              X-treme Solution   17

Chapter 4   One Maniacal Mabel and
              a Pumped Up Principal   23

Chapter 5   A New Kind of Track Team
              and a Cry for Help   33

Chapter 6   A Slick Diversion and One
              Big Brain   41

Chapter 7   One Quality Hotel and
              a Giant Fraud   47

Chapter 8   Two Big Brains and a
              Perfect Solution   53

Chapter 9   A Mesmerizing Madam and
              a New Ninja Warrior   63

Chapter 10   Crouching Principal,
              Hidden Warrior   69

Chapter 11   Strength, Brains, and
              One Cool Cuz   77

THINKING ROOM RULES

NO FOOD OR DRINK

KEEP HANDS TO YOURSELF

NO STANDING OR THROWING FURNITURE

CHAPTER 1

The Thinking Room and Two Wrongly Accused Dudes

So there I sat, stuck in The Thinking Room with a bunch of kids who aren't right. You don't believe me? Bet. This one girl just took the can of Lysol off Mr. Haycock's desk and told him if he didn't let her go to the bathroom for the fourth time, she was gonna spray it in his face!

Mr. Haycock is one tough dude. His job is to keep the Thinking Room under control. He used to be the gym teacher until he was demoted to In-School-Suspension warden by a three-time Olympic champ who replaced him.

A'lo's in here with me. He seems to be doing all right. Dude is sleeping just like he does in regular class. A'lo can be low down, but he saved me last week, and I owe him one for sure.

So far, fifth-grade had been one weird year. It wasn't a bit fair that I got sent to the Thinking Room. I was as mad as when you lose a 1-v-4 and your teammates loot your prizes, but you won't believe what happened next.

Hold up. Let me introduce myself. Everybody calls me Big Monty, but my real name is Merlin Montgomery. Go ahead. Get your laughs in about the name Merlin. But before you go getting too funny, just remember that haircut your mama gave you back in kindergarten. That style is documented for eternity in the school yearbook, and by eternity, I mean people can see it FOREVER! From here on out, anybody can find your ridiculous homemade-haircut-looking head.

MONEDERO   MERLIN MONTGOMERY   ROSE MU

Sorry about the haircut crack. I'm kind of touchy about my name. If you'd call me Big Monty, we'd be straight. I'm just ticked off because I'm stuck for the second day in a row in the Thinking Room instead of my regular classroom. The Thinking Room is some name they gave In-School-Suspension, so the parents don't get too hot when their kids get sent there. The place is trash. All you do in the Thinking Room is sit there, do your work, and think about what you did to get sent there.

You know the worst part? I'm being punished for saving my entire class! If it weren't for me and A'lo Jenkins, a bunch of fifth graders would still be frozen by that misguided substitute teacher, Colonel Freeze. By misguided I mean he thought he could impress kids by trying to be funny and cool and then got mad when they laughed at him. I'm not talking regular mad. That dude had a secret weapon where his false arm should have been that froze kids solid.

A'lo and I tried to freeze The Freeze with a fire extinguisher. Our plan went way wrong, but we ended up talking the guy into being the best sub at Washington Carver. Still, all the school wants to focus on is the fact that we snuck into the science closet and made a big mess in the hallway (read *Big Monty and the Cyborg Substitute* to find out about that story). That's what got us thrown into the Thinking Room, but, like I said, you won't believe what happened next.

———————

Smoke Ring Cannon

Here's a smoke-filled science experiment you can do at home that won't get you in trouble, as long as your parents help you with the matches. I found it on the website for Science Magazine — https://www. sciencefocus.com/science/how-to-make-a-smoke-ring-cannon/

Why am I telling you this? Because if you put down information in writing that isn't your own and don't tell where you found it, that's called plagiarism. And plagiarism will definitely get you sent to the Thinking Room! Plus, it's just not cool to finesse somebody's else's ideas.

What you'll need:

One-liter plastic bottle

Scissors

Rubber balloon

Sticky tape

Incense stick

Matches

Warning: This experiment involves a naked flame, so it should be carried out with adult supervision.

What to do:

1. Use scissors to cut off the bottom third of the plastic bottle.

2. Cut the balloon at the base of the neck. Discard the neck and keep the main round section.

3. Stretch the balloon over the open bottom of the bottle, so that it forms a tight 'skin'.

4. Secure the balloon to the sides of the bottle with sticky tape.

5. Light an incense stick.

6. Hold the open neck of the bottle directly above the burning incense stick until the bottle is full of smoke.

7. To make smoke rings, tap or poke the balloon skin with your fingers. Varying how hard you tap or poke will give different results.

CHAPTER 2

A Superior Substitute and One Weird Inmate

So there I sat in a desk small enough for a first-grader, feeling sorry for myself, when Principal Williams walked into the Thinking Room and pointed to his watch. Our three-piece-suit-wearing administrator said, "Time for your doctor's appointment Mr. Haycock?"

Mr. Haycock quickly threw his *Sports Scores* magazine into his desk drawer. "Thank you, Mr. Williams. All of the students have finished their work except Mr. Jenkins, who is sleeping, and Ms. Mabel who is more focused on trips to the bathroom."

"No problem," Mr. Williams said, straightening his tie. "I can handle them. Go ahead to your appointment. I've got this bunch covered."

Mr. Haycock tucked the tail of his shirt into his Big and Tall pants and lumbered toward the Thinking Room door. He paused before leaving, "Principal Williams, watch that Lysol with Mabel."

Principal Williams saluted Mr. Haycock like they were running some kind of military op. Then, he walked over to A'lo's desk and picked up a fat math book. The principal raised the book above A'lo's desk and SMACK! Dropped it right beside his sleeping head.

Dude shot up out of his seat all wild eyed with a dent in his hair that made his head look lopsided. His fists were balled up like he was ready to fight Mr. Williams. It took him a minute to remember where he was. "Mr. Jenkins," said Principal Williams. "Care to join us for a little learning today?"

A'lo slumped back down into his desk and opened his math book, grumbling under his breath about, "Tuxedo-wearin', penquin-looking, mom-callin' principals."

Mr. Williams ignored A'lo and gave him a freshly sharpened pencil. Then, he moved down the row to deal with Mabel. Mabel wore a brand new Goochie hoodie pulled over her basketball-shaped head. Bet. That

thing was perfectly round. Mabel was sup-
posed to be in second grade, but she tested
like some kind of genius and got moved up
to fifth grade right before winter break. They
obviously didn't test her on behavior. Uh-oh.
"This should be good," I thought.

"Ms. Mabel," began Principal Williams.
"What is the issue with the bathroom?"

"You can't tell me I can't go to the bathroom," she spat, peeking out of her hoodie
with beady little eyes you could hardly see
because her hair hung down over them. "I
have female problems."

"Female problems? The last time you said
you had female problems, we had to file a

missing person's report on you!" Principal Williams turned red for a minute.

"It's illegal to keep kids from going when they got to use it," she hissed.

Principal Williams leaned down and reached into Mabel's backpack. "Maybe you wouldn't have to use it so much if you quit drinking so many of these!" He held up three crushed cans of Superhuman X-treme Energy drinks.

"Dude," A'lo said from the back of the room, "I heard one of those can stop your heart. No freakin' wonder."

"That's enough Mr. Jenkins. Get back to your work." Principal Williams carried the three empties and the last remaining full can of Superhuman X-treme to the front of the room. He tossed the empty cans in the trash and put the unopened drink on the corner of the desk. Mr. Williams sat down in Mr. Haycock's seat and calmly said, "Mabel, you may go to the bathroom one last time. Then, you need to begin your work unless you would like another day in the Thinking Room."

Mabel went, arms and head jerking like a floundering fish, and the room got quiet.

Mabel's mom let her drink Superhuman X-treme Energy Drinks, but my mama only lets us drink one thing - water. I used to beg her for fizzy drinks filled with caffeine and sugar, until I watched that YouTube video about kids' teeth rotting out of their heads by the time they were 16 years old!

Know what else? Energy drinks, sports drinks, and Cokes cause diabetes. You can bet I don't want high blood sugar like my Grandpa P. If you replace drinking one sports drink or soda a day with drinking a glass of water, you would reduce enough calories and sugar in a year to lose 20 lbs (lbs means pounds)!

So, here's my challenge to you: see if you can drink three full glasses of water every day for the next week and skip the sugar drink. Or, fill up a large water bottle with ice and water and try and drink the whole thing by the end of the day. I know they make all those other drinks seem cool on TV, but water is where it's at.

CHAPTER 3

A Sleep Fighter and an X-treme Solution

Mabel twitched back into The Thinking Room and slapped the stack of worksheets Principal Williams handed her on top of her desk. As she jerked into her seat, her hands shook worse than the old folks at Grandma P's assisted living home.

I pulled out my copy of *Death by Black Hole* and put it in my lap under my desk. A black hole is a place in space where gravity pulls so hard that even light can't get out. Gravity is the force that keeps our feet on the ground and stops us from floating like LeBron James. Did you know if you fall into a black hole, your feet would fall faster than your head? Dude. That is an ugly way to die.

Maybe another half a day in the Thinking Room wouldn't be so bad. I was deep into reading about how a black hole would literally snap your body into two pieces, when

THUNK! I looked up and Principal Williams was rubbing his head where it had slammed on the desk when he fell asleep for a minute.

A'lo snorted.

"Hush!" Mr. Williams snapped, shaking his head from side to side and rubbing his eyes.

Principal Williams seemed to revive himself for a few minutes. I watched him lay his head in his hand, elbow propped up on the desk. This was a position I had seen A'lo take almost daily since Kindergarten, and I knew it wouldn't be long. I glanced back at A'lo who was grinning like a possum eating a sweet potato, as my Grandma P. would say. He knew what was coming too. We were about to see gravity in action.

First, Principal William's eyes started to flutter. Then they shut completely. His mouth fell open against the side of his palm. Within a minute, a string of drool snuck down his chin and swung there between his face and the desk.

"Five," whispered A'lo. "Four," he said, as the drool stretched. "Three," the end of the spit trail was just centimeters from the desk. "Two, One!" A'lo called out loudly as the drool landed SLURP on Mr. Haycock's desk.

Principal Williams jumped up and wiped his face with his sleeve. He looked helplessly from the class of lunatics to the clock on the wall. Two more hours. I could see the wheels in his head turning. How would he ever stay awake for two more hours in this jail cell—I mean, Thinking Room?

He paced back and forth in front of the room a few times, and his gaze fell on the Superhuman X-treme Energy drink on the corner of the teacher's desk. Principal Williams glanced around to see if anyone was looking, and snuck the can up his suit coat sleeve. "Class, I'm just going to step out in the hall for one minute," he said.

I'm about to nerd-out and talk more about gravity. Here's a trick question: Do heavier objects fall faster than lighter ones? Like if you dropped a bowling ball and a tennis ball from your roof, which would hit the ground first? Don't do that, your mama would freak.

Aiight, go try it, not on the roof. Stand on a porch or a playhouse and drop something light and something heavy at the same time. Which one hits the ground first?

Surprised? Now, Google it and find out which law of gravity is at work. And don't let any of your cousins like A'lo make you feel bad for learning. Let's say it again for the people in the back, "Smart equals successful!" Amen.

CHAPTER 4

One Maniacal Mabel and a Pumped Up Principal

We all perked up as we listened to Principal Williams pop the top on Mabel's drink and GLUNK! GLUNK! GLUNK! We heard him chug down the entire can just outside the door.

As the can fell to the floor, Ernesto Chavez yelled, "Ay Dios Mio. Oh my God! He drank it!"

"Bruh. Even my momma don't let me drink that stuff, and she thinks hot fries are a vegetable," A'lo said.

I looked around the Thinking Room at the rest of the inmates. Even clueless Clayton Claborne, who only cares about Fortnite and recess, seemed to know something BAD was about to happen. Mabel started to laugh like some kind of crazed hyena. She shook so hard that she fell out of her desk onto the floor.

"Man down!" cried Ernesto.

Principal Williams stuck his head through the doorway, "What's going on in here?"

He bent over Mabel and tried to pick her up by her armpits, but she wiggled like an eel on a hook and flopped back to the floor. "Mabel, return to your seat immediately!"

When Principal Williams stood up, there were sweat beads rolling down the side of his head. He loosened his tie.

"You," Mabel croaked between hyena screeches, "Are in," she struggled to breathe, "deep doo-doo!" she squealed.

"Lord have mercy," I thought. "What has Mabel done to the man with her toxic energy drink?"

"It starts with a heat in the belly!" screeched Mabel, who was crawling to her knees to better enjoy the spectacle that had become Principal Williams. And by spectacle, I mean he was making a complete fool of himself.

Principal Williams normally walked around looking totally refined, like he was going to an important dinner at The White House. All of a sudden, he started clawing at his pants like when my sister Josephine stepped in a pile of fire ants at Grandpa P's farm last summer.

I got out of my seat and moved to the back next to A'lo. If anything went down, you definitely wanted to be near that little gangster. The rest of the kids started to follow me, all except Mabel, who was crawling around and laughing like some creature from a horror movie.

Then, the unthinkable happened. Principal Williams, the man who won Principal of the Year for the last three years in our state, ripped off his pants! And you won't believe what we saw. That man had on Rey Mysterio's blue tights with the words, "Go Hard!" written on the leg.

At first, everybody went crazy laughing, but then, Mr. Williams lurched toward us like something off *The Walking Dead*. He grabbed the light fixture above Mabel's head, swung both legs around and took her out with Mysterio's famous move The 619!

"Ooooooooooo," all twelve of the kids in the Thinking Room winced. Principal Williams tossed her across the room all twisted up like a pretzel and looked around at the rest of us.

"Run!" yelled A'lo, and since everybody always listens to that big-mouth, we ran.

Yo. You ready to find out what happened to Prinicpal William's heart rate when he drank the Superhuman X-treme Energy drink? When you do something like exercise, or get nervous, or drink an energy drink, your pulse, or heart rate speeds up.

Let's find your heart rate. I found this activity – https://www.scienceforkidsclub.com/heart-experiment.html

Here is what you need:

Yourself
Pen and paper
The help of an adult
Stop watch, timer with seconds, or clock with a second hand

Here is what you do:

1. Get familiar with checking your heart rate

   To check your heart rate, put your first two fingers just below your jaw; pressing GENTLY and feeling for the spot where you can feel your pulse. If you are having trouble, ask a parent to help you.

   Once you are confident you can check your pulse or have someone do it for you, continue with the remaining steps in this experiment.

   Standing still, take your heart rate by counting how many times your heart beats in 15 seconds. Then multiply that number by 4 to get the number of beats per minute. Write it down.

2. Run in place for one minute, stop, take your heart rate, and write down the number of beats per minute.

3. Lie down for one minute, take your heart rate, and write down the number of beats per minute.

4. Walk around your house at a normal pace for one minute, take your heart rate, and write down the number of beats per minute.

Look at the results—

- When did your heart beat the fastest?
- When did it beat the slowest?
- What was your highest heart rate?
- What was your slowest heart rate?

CHAPTER 5

A New Kind of Track Team and a Cry for Help

For someone who is way out of shape, A'lo was quick to lead the pack of Thinking Room inmates straight down the hall to the gym. Even dumpy Tyson Magee and the kid without any shoelaces moved pretty fast. I was right on A'lo's heel, but I paused to wave my arms in front of my sister Josephine's classroom. Teachers listened to kids like Josephine. Maybe she could get us some help.

My sister was wearing her usual polka-dotted bows, sitting in the front row with her hand jetting up in the poor teacher's face. Josephine never let anyone beat her to an answer. I banged on the window and motioned like someone was strangling me. She turned around and squinted her smart little eyes like she wanted to say, "Why are you interrupting my learning time?" I pointed frantically down the hall. Principal Williams came thundering around the corner, so I had to keep moving.

I passed the pack of Thinking Room degenerates and caught up with A'lo, who was sprinting to the gym. I guessed he was hoping Coach Hamhock would put a beatdown on our pumped-up principal. Coach Hamhock was a three-time Olympic Deadlift Champion who could take on any fool, even one hopped up on toxic energy drink. Unfortunate circumstances during her fourth Olympic tryouts led her to Washington Carver Elementary (read *Big Monty and the Lunatic Lunch Lady* to find out about that story).

We all pushed through the double doors and hurled ourselves into the gym. Principal Williams was salivating and closing in on Ernesto. "Ayúdame! Help me!" cried Ernesto. On God, Principal Williams grabbed the back of his shirt, picked Ernesto up over his head, and perfected a Gorilla Press Slam on the kid!

"Ooooooo!" All the Thinking Room kids froze in their tracks across the empty gym floor.

Next, Principal Williams came after the boy with no shoelaces and put him in a straight-up Texas Cloverleaf hold. The kid's veins bulged on his forehead and he started gasping for breath.

"Where's Hamhock?" A'lo's dark eyes darted all around the gym, but it was deserted.

"Maybe she took the class out to the soft-ball fields," I said.

Principal Williams was tying kids up and slamming them left and right. A'lo and I were circling the edge of the gym with our backs against the wall. All of a sudden, the plexiglass window behind us shot open and my sister's polka-dot painted fingernails reached over the ledge. She pulled her bow-clad head over the windowsill and said, "Merlin, I just texted Global's sister, and she said Mad Hatter Magee is in town staying at Global's hotel."

Global has been my best friend since kindergarten. Kid is mad smart and wicked funny, but he wears brown socks and the same pants he's worn since the second grade. His family owns a hotel in downtown Memphis near the Pyramid. You can see the Mississippi river from the third floor.

"Mad Hatter Magee? Here?" I said. What would a WWE wrestling star be doing at Global's hotel?

"Are you goofy?" said A'lo as Principal Williams put a Python Squeeze on this skinny girl, "Don't you know there's a wrestling expo at the Fed-ex Forum Saturday night?"

"Mad Hatter's mom lives in Memphis, but she won't let him come visit her because she says it's a disgrace that he wears underwear on TV for a living," Josephine said.

"How do you guys know all this?" I said.

"Bruh, everybody follows Mad Hatter on TikTok," A'lo said. "What kind of nerdy planet are you living on?" Typical A'lo. And to think, for a few days, I actually thought about liking this little big-mouth.

"Speaking of," said Josephine. "I'm up to 570,000 followers."

Principal Williams had put down every kid from the Thinking Room and was coming straight for us. "You better go get Mad Hatter to stop this wannabe!" Josephine yelled.

"Stay close," said A'lo. We huddled together in front of the window until Principal Williams put his head down and charged us like a furious bull.

At the last second, I dove right and A'lo went left. Josephine slammed the unbreakable plexiglass shut. Principal Williams hit the window like a dodgeball, and he went down. He was out stone cold, and we ran to find Global.

Tag Matt Maxx on Insta or FB at @ mattmaxxbooks with a picture of yourself reading, writing, or drawing!

CHAPTER 6

A Slick Diversion and One Big Brain

Global sat at the audio center in our classroom, wearing too-short brown pants with huge headphones clamped over his ears.

"I'll distract Ms. Pinkerton, and you get Global," said A'lo.

A'lo strutted into our classroom like a miniature mob boss and announced, "Ms. Pinkerton, I've decided to get serious about my studies."

Now, Ms. Pinkerton was one of those special elementary school teachers who lived for students. She spent gobs of her own money on materials for our class, took us on field trips that were actually fun *and* educational, and came to see our basketball games on Saturday mornings. Ms. Pinkerton had been trying all year to get A'lo Jenkins interested in school, but that was like trying to get an alligator interested in eating salads.

"You're what?" Ms. Pinkerton's eyes lit up and she practically knocked over Slim Smith as she ran to A'lo and hugged him.

"I'm ready to get serious," A'lo said with a face straight as an ironing board.

You had to admit, A'lo might not have been into school, but that dude was smart! I snuck behind them, grabbed Global by his chubby shoulders and dragged him with me out of the classroom.

"What are you doing, Big Monty-Merlin?" Global's eyes looked even bigger through his thick glasses. He was the only kid in school who even tried to remember my nickname, but he never got it quite right, no matter how many times I reminded him.

"Global, is it true that Mad Hatter Magee is staying at your family's hotel?"

"Mad Hatter, the celebrated television athlete?"

"Yeah man, the WWE professional wrestler!" Global never missed more than one question on a test, but he didn't know normal stuff like sports scores or which movies were good.

"Yes, I believe he has been there since Tuesday."

"Awesome, we've got to go get him. Principal Williams has gone ham on the students from the Thinking Room. He needs to meet his match on the mat."

"I am not allowed to fraternize with patrons of the hotel, Big Monty-Merlin." By fraternize, Global means talk to or hang out with guests.

"Global, this is an emergency. Principal Williams has turned into some kind of crazed wrestler and is throwing kids all over the school gym. We've got to stop him before he really hurts someone and gets fired. You wouldn't want some below-average principal to replace him. Would you?"

"Definitely not. I need his reputation intact for my college recommendation letters," said Global.

I'd finally gotten through to that seriously smart dude. We cruised out of the emergency exit and down the road past St. Jude's.

We all know Global is a little off the chain about going to college. He's had a resume since second grade. A resume is a paper that tells colleges and employers what skills you have and why they would want to hire you or accept you into their school. I'll show you how to make one, then you can send me yours at whoismattmaxx@gmail.com.

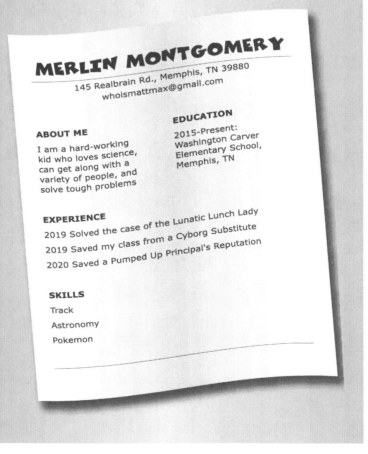

MERLIN MONTGOMERY

145 Realbrain Rd., Memphis, TN 39880
whoismattmax@gmail.com

ABOUT ME

I am a hard-working kid who loves science, can get along with a variety of people, and solve tough problems

EDUCATION

2015-Present: Washington Carver Elementary School, Memphis, TN

EXPERIENCE

2019 Solved the case of the Lunatic Lunch Lady
2019 Saved my class from a Cyborg Substitute
2020 Saved a Pumped Up Principal's Reputation

SKILLS

Track

Astronomy

Pokemon

CHAPTER 7

One Quality Hotel
and a Giant Fraud

Global sucked wind as we jogged the eight blocks down the road to the Quality Hotel. We snuck past Global's Aunt Anayah, and knocked on Mad Hatter's door. No one answered, but we heard the television blaring Disney songs.

"Is he watching Frozen?" I said, banging on the door again. Someone fumbled around, and then a short man with a bushy beard wearing a bathrobe answered the door.

"Hello, Sir. Are you the wrestler known as Mad Hatter Magee?" Global shook his hand like a young governor campaigning for re-election.

"I am," the man puffed out his chest and shook Global's hand so hard he almost came out of his off-brand tennis shoes.

"We are here to request your assistance at Washington Carver Elementary School. My friend Merlin just witnessed our very fine principal ingest a toxic energy drink called 'Superhuman X-treme.' He is presently under the delusion that he is a professional wrestler and is attacking students in the gym."

"Superhuman X-treme?" said Mad Hatter. "Nobody drinks that stuff!"

"You do," I said. "Before every match!"

"Not in real life, kid. That stuff is toxic!" Mad Hatter pulled the bathrobe around him. "Listen kids, I hate to disappoint you, but I'm not a real wrestler. That stuff on TV is just for show."

"But the Thornbuster Drop?" I said in disbelief. I'd seen him take much bigger guys out with this move dozens of times on Saturday morning TV.

"Pure acting genius," Mad Hatter shook his head.

I hadn't been so disappointed since Grandma P. took out her teeth and showed me they weren't real. "Well, you're still really strong. You ought to be able to take our principal on."

"Sorry boys, I'm hanging up my wrestling tights. I miss my mom, and she thinks I am wasting my life. I've come back to Memphis to start a new career. I'll be teaching ballet at Dancing Divine starting Monday." Mad Hatter pushed us out the door and closed it in our faces.

There are a lot of fakes and frauds out there who sell things they don't really believe in or even use. Draw an example of a commercial you've seen with a famous athlete, actress, or singer where they are selling or endorsing a product. How are they trying to get you to want to buy it? Let me see your cartoon skills at Mattmaxxbooks on FB or IG! Get your parents to take a picture and I'll post it!

CHAPTER 8

Two Big Brains and a Perfect Solution

I was shaken like a magnitude 7 earthquake. "Mad Hatter's a fraud and Principal Williams has lost his doggone mind."

"I had a feeling," said Global. "Those wrestlers are not the most convincing performers

I have ever seen. As my taekwondo teacher tells us each week, 'It is not the size of the dog in the fight, it's the size of the fight in the dog.'"

"Global, that's it! Aren't you like a brown belt in kung-fu? You can take on Principal Williams!"

"As a matter of fact, I just received my black belt, Big Monty-Merlin. But, I do not believe my skills could vanquish a grown man on artificial stimulants." By that, Global meant he didn't think he could win against a principal pumped-up on deadly amounts of caffeine and sugar.

"A black belt? That's awesome," I said, as the glass-fronted building on Syner-Genetics Laboratories caught my eye about half-a-mile down the road. "Mad Hatter was a fake. But, you know who's the real deal?" I asked Global. "My dad."

Global followed my gaze toward my dad's building and his eyes lit up. "Are we going to Syner-Genetics?" he squealed.

"Calm down, Man," I told him. "I'm sure my dad can help us figure out how to harness your karate skills and save Principal William's reputation."

We high-tailed it six blocks down the street toward the monstrous science mecca. Syner-Genetics is the leading research company on cloning in the United States. Last year, my dad brought home a picture of a successful Platy-potamus hybrid. If he could figure out how to combine a hippo with a platypus, maybe he could inject Global with the courage of a ferocious beast. We needed to match Global's taekwondo skills with some untamed passion.

My dad stood bent over a microscope looking into a petri dish when we entered his lab. "Ooooo! Can I look?" Global shrieked.

"Hey guys, what brings you here this hour of day?" my dad said as he stepped aside and motioned to Global to look through the microscope. Global practically knocked me down in his excitement to inspect whatever it was in that petri dish.

"Dad, I need your help," I said. "Principal Williams is all jazzed up on this Superhuman X-treme Energy drink. He's tossing the students around and is about to lose his reputation and his job."

"Drinking unstable substances has probable risks Principal Williams should have foreseen," my dad said. Sometimes, I think Global and I were switched at birth.

"Here's the deal. Global has the martial arts skills to slam the energy out of Principal Williams, but he lacks the courage to defeat him," I said. "If you could inject Global with the DNA of a lion, maybe we have a chance at saving Principal William's job."

"Son, I'm afraid to inform you that on rare occasions science does reach its limits." My dad got a far away look in his eyes. "Courage is one of those elusive qualities that is beyond the reach of genetics." By elusive, he means it's hard to understand or figure out.

Dad put his arm on my shoulder and said, "Courage is not a matter of biology. It's a matter of psychology, but that is not my field."

My dad and Global used a microscope to see things you can't see with the naked eye. Ha ha—I know, *naked* cracks me up, too. But it just means your regular eyes without a microscope or telescope or other tool to magnify objects. Here are some cool experiments you can do with your naked eye that I found at https://learning-center. homesciencetools.com.

Blind Spot Experiments

Do you know you have a blind spot? We all do. You don't notice this blind spot in every-day life, because your two eyes work together to cover it up.

To find it, draw a filled-in 1/4" square and a circle three or four inches apart on a piece of white paper.

Hold the paper at arm's length and close your left eye. Focus on the square with your right eye, and slowly move the paper toward you. When the circle reaches your blind spot, it will disappear!

Try again to find the blind spot for your other eye. Close your right eye and focus on the circle with your left eye. Move the paper until the square disappears.

What happened when the shape disappeared? Did you see nothing where the shape had been?

No, when the shape disappeared, you saw a plain white background that matched the rest of the sheet of paper.

This is because your brain "filled in" for the blind spot – your eye didn't send any information about that part of the paper, so the brain just made the "hole" match the rest.

Try the experiment again on a piece of colored paper. When the circle disappears, the brain will fill in whatever color matches the rest of the paper.

The brain doesn't just match colored backgrounds. It can also make other changes to what you see. Try drawing two filled-in rectangles side by side with a circle in between them. A few inches to the right of this, draw a square.

Close your right eye and focus your left eye on the square. Move the paper until the circle disappears and the two separated bars become one bar.

How did that happen? The circle in between the bars fell on your blind spot. When it disappeared, the brain filled in for the missing information by connecting the two bars!

Here is one final experiment with your blind spot. In this instance, the brain doesn't match the blind spot with its immediate white background, but instead, it matches with the pattern surrounding it.

Draw a line down the center of your page. On one side, draw a small square, and on the other, draw rows of circles. Color the center circle red and all the others blue.

Close your left eye and look at the square with your right eye. As you move the paper, the red circle should disappear and be replaced by a blue one!

CHAPTER 9

A Mesmerizing Madam and a New Ninja Warrior

As we walked out of Syner-Genetics Laboratory, I thought about what my dad said. Under the right psychological conditions, Global's skills could be powerful enough to take down Principal Williams.

But how were we going to change Global's mentality in time to save our school from total humiliation?

Just then, we passed Madam Fu Fu's House of Hypnosis. "I've got it! Global, come on, Bro." I grabbed that awkward dude's arm and dragged him up the crumbling sidewalk to the purple two-story building.

We rang the doorbell that sounded like a moose breaking wind. Madam Fu Fu stuck her pasty face to the window in the door. She wore lipstick all over her mouth and purple eyeshadow, which matched her house, almost up to her hairline.

"Madam Fu Fu," I said in my loud voice, "we need your help!" She narrowed her eyes, listening as I told her about Global's need for courage that matched his martial arts skills.

Then, faster than you can build your 90s, Madam Fu Fu had Global's eyes rolling around in his head while she swung a crystal necklace inches from his nose. "You're getting very sleepy," she croaked in her frog voice. "Very, very sleepy." Global looked like a bug-eyed parrot swaying his head back and forth with the necklace. "I will count down from ten, and when I get to one, you will have fighting skills like Conor McGregor."

For a minute, I wanted to switch places with Global. Conor McGregor was one tough dude. I could just picture myself taking out that sixth-grader, Slim Tez, who stole my seat on the bus every morning.

Madame Fu Fu counted down, and on "one," she snapped her bony fingers, and Global stood up, straight as a soldier. All of a sudden, instead of chubby, that dude looked thick and powerful.

"Merlin," whispered Madam Fu Fu, "When you want to bring him back to normal, you have to say, 'greens, beans, potatoes, tomatoes, lambs, rams, hogs, dogs."

"All of that?" I asked, and she nodded as I led my new fighting machine back to the streets.

Madam Fu Fu has her tricks, but let me teach you one of mine. I won five bucks off of A'lo on this one!

On all six-sided dice, the opposite sides add up to 7. So, you can tell your friend, "I bet I can guess what number is face-down every time you roll that dice."

Then, if they roll a four, you know the opposite side of the dice that is facing down has to be the number that you add to four to get to seven. Three!

If they roll a two, the opposite side has to be a five to add to seven.

Try it!

CHAPTER 10

Crouching Principal, Hidden Warrior

Aside from the physical change, Global seemed pretty normal to me. In fact, I couldn't tell he was hypnotized at all. He just kept rambling about the subatomic particles he saw in that petri dish in my dad's lab.

"Global, you understand saving the school is all on you, right?" I asked my genius friend.

"Oh yes. I am quite sure that by leveraging the physics of balance and counterbalance, I can subdue Principal Williams with very little harm." Global said, as if he did this kind of thing every weekend.

We walked straight in through the front doors of Washington Carver Elementary. The office doors were wide open with papers scattered everywhere. It looked like a Tasmanian devil had whirled through the front of the school. Furniture was turned upside down, and the hallways were deserted.

All of a sudden, my sister Josephine stuck her head out of the library, "Pssst! Down here," she hissed.

Global puffed his chest out like a prize-fighter and led the way. I have to admit, I was pretty proud to be Global's wing-man at that moment. He looked almost . . . cool.

Global kicked the door open. We stood ten yards away from Principal Williams, who was squatting on top of a bookshelf with his head almost touching the ceiling.

His eyes darted back and forth like a hawk searching for prey. Kids were cowering under tables, and the librarian, Mrs. Anthony, had locked herself in her office. I could see her through the glass window piling a fortress of books around her.

Global walked boldly forward into the Biography section and stood right under Principal Williams' furious gaze. Never in a million years would I have guessed what Global would do next. He pushed his glasses up his nose, began beating his chest with his fists, and ROARED like the king of the jungle.

I yelled out, "Say hello to my little friend!"

Principal Williams leaped off the bookshelf and charged straight for Global. With one swift move, Global pivoted, stuck his foot out as slick as a fox, and BAM! Principal Williams kissed the floor so hard, I thought he'd be lipless for the rest of his life. Global spun like a thoroughbred stallion and galloped straight toward our dazed administrator. He grabbed Principal Williams in a grappling hold. The man's face went pale, his eyes closed, and he slumped into Global's arms.

"Global! Enough! You're killing him!" I cried. "Greens, beans, tomatoes..."

"Relax Big Monty-Merlin. I simply executed a Rear Naked Hold that reduces blood from passing through his arteries. The amount of pressure applied isn't fatal. It only restricts the amount of oxygen to the brain. I am completely aware of his physical state and will release the choke at the first signs of loss of consciousness." Global looked as calm and confident as Kawhi Leonard in a kids' rec league game, but he still sounded like his old geeky self.

"You did it, Man!" Prinipal Williams slept like an overgrown baby as Global loosened his hold.

Global defeated Principal Williams by using physics and balance. Here's a trick for you using the same principles.

Hold up. Josephine wants me to tell you something. She says to tell you, "When you spell it 'principal,' it means the leader of a school. When you spell it 'principle,' it means a set of ideas, facts, or rules. Words like these that are spelled differently but sound the same are homophones."

Ok, back to the project. Take your mama's broomstick outside and see if you can balance the stick on the palm of your hand. Any luck? Probably not.

Now do the same thing, but look up at the top of the broom and move your hand and feet around and see what you can do. Longer? Yup. Now try it on the end of one finger.

Now try it with a ladder. Yo, I'm joking! A broom is impressive enough, Dude!

According to www.jugglingworld.biz, The secret to balancing is simply to watch the very top of the object. Watching the object at the base tells you nothing about where it is likely to fall, whereas the top of the object moves around in a much wider arc and gives you much more visual clues which your brain can interpret and co-ordinate with your body to keep the object upright!

CHAPTER 11

Strength, Brains, and One Cool Cuz

Lucky for Principal Williams, he didn't lose his job. Because of his outstanding reputation, he only received two weeks of suspension. I guess that's the adult version of the Thinking Room.

The first thing Principal Williams did when he returned to school was hang posters in every hallway, classroom, and bathroom that said, "ABSOLUTELY NO ENERGY DRINKS ALLOWED AT SCHOOL!"

The second thing he did was call Global and me into his office. "Gentleman," he said, straightening his tie. "I'd like to thank you for using your brains and your brawn to subdue a volatile situation."

"A commendation is not necessary, Sir," said Global. By *commendation*, Global means a prize or recognition for saving Principal Williams. "Everyone knows you are an outstanding educator under normal circumstances."

"Everyone also knows you have a strange obsession with WWE now, too," I thought but did not say out loud. What I did say was, "Everyone makes mistakes, Sir." I hoped this might keep me out of the Thinking Room next time something crazy happens at Washington Carver.

As Global and I left the office and walked down the hall toward Ms. Pinkerton's room, we passed A'lo in the hallway joking on Tyrone Ellis, "Your mama's so dumb, she sold her car for gas money. HAHA HAHA!"

Global stopped outside the door and turned to me. "Merlin, I mean, Big Monty, I want to thank you for leading me to Madam Fu Fu. She really unlocked my subconscious confidence."

"Please, Bro. Everyone knows Madam Fu Fu's a fake. She's no different from Mad Hatter. You had it in you all along," I said.

You know what really amazes me? As many facts as Global keeps in his head, he still had room for courage. Bet. Now that Global has street cred, if he would just remember to call me Big Monty, I might seriously get that name to catch on!

Hey Reader,

Matt Maxx here. I love seeing so many of you reading Big Monty books. Hey, Clifford Ray even read Big Monty for his online book club. Check him out! Jake, Ade, and Sam all sent great ideas for the next villain to me at whoismattmaxx@gmail. com. And my friend in Dallas used Big Monty for his story board report that his mom shared on the Insta page @mattmaxxbooks. Y'all are out there doing it! I love hearing from you and seeing your pictures. Keep sending them. And remember, you can find science experiments and free coloring books on my website at www.mattmaxxbooks.com.

Peace Out,
Matt Maxx

Made in the USA
Middletown, DE
06 July 2020

12094205R10054